Anonymous

Prophetic Conjectures on the French Revolution

and other recent and shortly expected events

Anonymous

Prophetic Conjectures on the French Revolution
and other recent and shortly expected events

ISBN/EAN: 9783337227357

Printed in Europe, USA, Canada, Australia, Japan

Cover: Foto ©Andreas Hilbeck / pixelio.de

More available books at **www.hansebooks.com**

PROPHETIC CONJECTURES

ON THE

FRENCH REVOLUTION.

[PRICE ONE SHILLING.]

PROPHETIC CONJECTURES

ON THE

FRENCH REVOLUTION,

AND OTHER RECENT

AND SHORTLY EXPECTED EVENTS:

EXTRACTED FROM

ARCHBP. BROWN . 1551	DR. H. MORE 1663
REV. J. KNOX 1572	REV. P. JURIEU . . . 1687
DR. T. GOODWIN . 1639	REV. R. FLEMING . 1701
REV. CHR. LOVE . 1651	REV. J. WILLISON . 1742
ARCHBP. USHER . 1655	DR. GILL 1748

AND

A REMARKABLE ANONYMOUS PAMPHLET, 1747.

WITH AN

INTRODUCTION AND REMARKS.

SURELY THE LORD GOD WILL DO NOTHING, BUT HE REVEALETH HIS SECRET UNTO HIS SERVANTS THE PROPHETS.   AMOS.

London:

PRINTED BY W. TAYLOR, SHOE MAKER ROW, BLACK FRIARS,

FOR WILLIAM BUTTON, No 24, PATERNOSTER ROW.

MDCCXCIII.

PROPHETIC CONJECTURES:

INTRODUCTION AND REMARKS:

INTRODUCTION.

PROPHECY is one of the best evidences of a divine revelation. And it is a peculiar glory of our Bible that it contains a regular series of prophecies from the earliest times to the consummation of all things. Even Enoch the seventh from Adam, prophesied: and though we have little preserved of that very early date, from the age of the flood we have a chain of Scripture predictions, which running through all the subsequent ages connects even with eternity. Noah foretold the manner in which the new world should be divided among his sons, and their different destinies. Abraham, Jacob and Moses, marked the out-lines of Jewish history down to the times of Messiah and later, with not a few circumstances relative to other nations. David greatly enlarged the treasures of inspiration; and the succeeding Prophets, each in clearer and fuller language, described the events of future and distant

B   ages

ages---the variou, revolutions of empires and
ftates--and fome of them even fixed the tin e in
which their words fhould be accomplifhed. The
New Teftament completes and illuftrates the Old.
Our Lord and his apoftle Paul added many valu-
able particulars; the former as to the clofe of the
Jewifh œconomy, and the latter with refpect to
the corruptions fince brought into the Chriftian
church. But the REVELATION of St. John, or
rather of *Jefus Chrift* to him, contains the moft full
and important feries of prophefies ever beftowed
on mankind; extending from the clofe of the firft
century of Chriftianity, about which period it was
written, to the end of time; and may be confidered
as an infpired comment on the predictions of
Daniel, referring in great meafure to the fame
events.

But prophecy was intended not *merely* as a confirmation of the divine records in which it was
contained; but alfo as a fource of comfort and encouragement to the Lord's people in times of
public diftrefs and danger; whence we find the
prophets particularly ftudied by good men in fuch
periods. It was during the feventy years captivity
that Daniel fearched the facred *books*, and found
that they were near expiring. It is highly probable that the ftudy of Daniel's prophecies prepared
the pious Jews for the coming of their Lord, after
having *waited for his falvation*, during a period of
great darknefs and depravity. And doubtlefs
many times when the Lord's people have been
looking out for deliverance to the church, *as thofe
that watch for the morning*, they have found much
encouragement for their hopes, and often wonderful and feafonable fulfilments of the divine pro-
mifes. It will be found, on enquiry, that moft of
· the

the authors from whom the following extracts are selected, wrote either during times of perfecution, or in the immediate profpect of them.

It is true, our Lord reproves thofe that were inquifitive as to *the times which the Father hath* referved *in his own power*; but it is no lefs obfervable, that he fharply accufed the Pharifees, for that they did not *difcern the figns of the times*. Secret things, indeed, *belong to the Lord our God; but thofe that are revealed, unto us and to our children.* To thefe REVEALED things (and fuch are the prophetic as well as other parts of fcripture) many great and good men have thought themfelves juftified in directing their humble and modeft enquiries; not without hopes that fome of thofe oracles, which the infpired inftruments who uttered them were not permitted to underftand, might yet be unveiled to others, in or near whofe times they were about to be accomplifhed; feeing the apoftle Peter teacheth us that *not unto themfelves, but unto us did they minifter the things which are reported* in the fcriptures. [See 1 Pet. i. 10--12.] It fhould not be thought ftrange and unaccountable, then, if fome fuggeftions of eminent and pious men fhould, remarkably correfpond with fubfequent events, and that even their *conjectures* fhould fometimes appear prophetic; efpecially as the *fecret of the Lord is with them that fear him*, and *he teacheth them wonderful things out of his* word. Surely it is not incredible, nor is it, I hope, enthufiaftic to fuppofe, that among the multitude of *rays* emitted from the *Sun of Righteoufnefs* to a believer who *walks in the light of his countenance*, fome may convey a peculiar infight to the fublime parts of fcripture; and after reading the enfuing paffages, I am perfuaded few will abfolutely deny the fact.

As

As this tract. may fall into the hands of some
persons but very little acquainted with the prophecies, and in particular with the Book of the
Revelation, on which most of the following conjectures are founded, it is judged necessary, in order
to render them intelligible, to prefix an idea of the
nature of the visions it contains, and a very brief
analysis of these prophesies, especially such parts of
them as are generally agreed to be already accomplished; and this shall be taken, for the most part,
from the 3d Vol. of the admirable and luminous
Dissertations of Bishop *Newton on the Prophecies.*

Let the reader, in the first place, observe, that the
visions which the beloved apostle relates in the
order in which he saw them, were emblematic re-
presentations of the future state of the church of
Christ, and of her enemies, in the various successive
ages of the world. It is not altogether agreed
whether the epistles to the seven churches in chap.
ii. and iii. were properly *prophetic* or not; but if
they were, it is supposed, 1. That the church of
Ephesus, represents the church in the apostolic age--
2. That of *Smyrna*, the time of the ten early per-
secutions, and to the days of Constantine---3.
That of *Pergamos*, the church from that period
during the rise of popery--4. That of *Thyatira*,
the dark ages of the church preceding the reform-
ation--5. That of *Sardis*, the reformed church--
6. That of *Philadelphia*, Christ's spiritual reign--and
the 7th and last, That of *Laodicea*, a state of remarkable declension expected to follow the latter
period, and immediately to precede the end of the
world. These are the ideas of the learned Dr.
Gill and others. What follows is chiefly (as we
proposed) from Bishop Newton.

Chap.

Chap. IV. and V. contain the *preparatory* vifion, in which is introduced a volume fealed with feven feals, which the Son of God alone is found able to unloofe.

Chap. VI. VII. and VIII. relate the opening of the SEALS, and the unfolding of the book, wherein

    " Each op'ning leaf, and ev'ry ftroke
    " Fulfils fome deep defign."

The *firft feal* opens a fcene of triumph, and is referred to a feries of remarkable victories obtained by the Romans, from the acceffion of Vefpafian to the reign of Nerva, inclufive; a period of not quite thirty years; which includes, however, the conqueft and deftruction of Jerufalem. This period was equally remarkable for the fucceffes of the gofpel, and to thofe fome chufe rather to refer this fcene.

The *fecond feal* introduces the bloody wars and flaughters which followed for near an hundred years, during the reigns of Trajan and his fucceffors down to Septimus Severus; including the rebellion and deftruction of the impoftor Barchochab, and his deluded followers,

The *third feal* defcribes the fevere juftice and œconomy which marked the reign of the laft mentioned emperor and his family, which continued for about forty years.

The *fourth feal* introduces a period of war, famine, peftilence, and the ravages of wild beafts; which lafted from the reign of Maximin to that of Dioclefian, about fifty years.

The *fifth feal* refers to what has been called the age of martyrs, the tenth and laft heathen perfecution under Dioclefian; which exceeded all the former, raging inceffantly for ten years.

The

The *fixth feal* ufhers in the grand revolution brought about by Conftantine, in which heathenifm was finally overthrown, and Chriftianity made the eftablifhed religion of the empire. This period is extended to the death of Theodofius, about feventy years, and brings us to near the clofe of the fourth century.

The *feventh* and laft *feal* introduces *feven* angels with *trumpets*, the founding of which fucceffively marks out feven other remarkable periods, which we have in Chap. VIII. and IX.

The *firft trumpet* defcribes the invafion of Alaric and the Goths, under the image of a tremendous ftorm.

The *fecond trumpet* reprefents the ravages of Attila and his Huns, by the figure of a burning mountain caft into the fea.

The *third trumpet* introduces the heretical Genferic and his Vandals from Italy, as a ftar falling from heaven, and embittering the waters.

The *fourth trumpet* refers to Odoacer and the Heruli, who totally deftroyed the poor remains of the Weftern Roman empire, even to the very name, and founded the kingdom of the Oftrogoths. This is reprefented in prophetic language as extinguifhing one third of the celeftial luminaries. Thefe events bring us to about the middle of the fixth century; and a proclamation is now made from heaven to prepare us for the three following, which are diftinguifhed by the name of *Wce* Trumpets, and introduce events ftill more terribly fublime.

The *fifth trumpet* introduces Mohammed, another fallen ftar, and his Arabian army, under the ftriking fimilitude of locufts.

The *fixth trumpet* lets loofe the four fultanies of Turks

Turks and Othmans, whofe wars are defcribed in tremendous language. Thefe trumpets effected the ruin of the Eaftern empire.

The *seventh trumpet* brings in the Millenium. But previous to this is introduced a fcene of a little book, which is confidered as a kind of appendix and illuftration of the preceding prophecies, and fome additions. This begins what is commonly called the *second part* of the Book of Revelation, which properly commences with the laft verfe of Chap. X.

Chap. XI. defcribes the character, death, and refurrection of God's faithful witneffes. Upon this chapter (particularly ver. 13.) great part of the following conjectures are founded; we fhall only apprize the reader that he will find authors not agreed whether the death and refurrection of thefe witneffes is yet paft or future. Thofe who maintain the former, explain it of fome of the following events, which remarkably coincide with the three prophetic days (or years) and an half; viz.

1. The feffion of the council of Conftance from November, 1414, to April, 1418, in which period Hufs and Jerom of Prague were burnt; after this the pope loft the kingdom of Bohemia.

2. The perfecution of the Proteftants of the league of Smalcald, from April, 1547, to December, 1550.

3. The perfecution of the cruel Q. Mary in England from Feb. 1555, to Nov. 1558.

4. From the maffacre of Paris, Sept. 1572, to the treaty of Henry III. of France in favor of the Hugonots, May, 1576, was nearly the fame period.

5. The popifh reign of our K. James II. from Feb. 1685, to Nov. 1688.

6. From the revocation of the edict of Nantz

in

in Oct. 1685, to the coronation of K. William III. in England, April, 1689, by which an afylum was in fome meafure provided for them, and their drooping hopes much encouraged.

7. From the cruel edict of the duke of Savoy againft the Proteftants in Piedmont, near the end of 1686, to another edict in their favor June, 1690:

8. Tyrconnel's viceroyfhip in Ireland under K. James II. from Feb. 1686-7, to K. William's victories in 1690.

All the above events and feveral others have been obferved to agree with the prediction in fome refpects; but none completely fo, its full accomplifhment waiting, perhaps, for fome event ftill future.

Chap. XII. defcribes a great red dragon, which is commonly underftood of Pagan Rome, and this vifion illuftrates the events of the firft fix feals.

Chap. XIII. 1--10. reprefents Papal Rome as a ten horned beaft, fucceffor to the preceding. Verfes 11--18. defcribes a two horned beaft, which Bifhop Newton and others explain of the Pope (called alfo the *falfe prophet*) and his clergy. The number of the beaft is explained with fome variety, but moft adopt the ancient notion of Ireneus who finds it in LATEINOS, the *Latin* or Roman, an epithet conftantly applied to the Weftern church; and it is remarkable that about this time (666) the ufe of *Latin* in the church offices became general. It is alfo obfervable that the Hebrew word ROMIITH, of the fame meaning as the Greek LATEINOS, contains alfo the fame number. Some writers fuppofe this beaft to mean the tyranny of the *Lewifes* in France, and therefore find the number in the numerals of LUDOVICUS, which anfwers to it in Latin. The truth of thefe matters may be feen as follows:

Λ	- -	30
Α	- -	1
Τ	-	300
Ε	- -	5
Ι	- -	10
Ν	- -	50
Ο	- -	70
Σ	- -	200
		666

ר	- -	200
ו	- -	6
מ	- -	40
י	- -	10
י	- -	10
ת	- -	400
		666

L	- -	50
V	- -	5
D	- -	500
O	- -	0
V	- -	5
I	- -	1
C	- -	100
V	- -	5
S	- -	0
		666

A late writer has also remarked, as a very singular circumstance, that the title VICARIUS FILII DEI, which the popes of Rome have assumed to themselves, and have caused, as is said, to be inscribed over the door of the Vatican, exactly makes the number 666, when decyphered.

V	- -	5
I	- -	1
C	- -	100
A	- -	0
R	- -	0
I	- -	1
V	- -	5
S	- -	0

F	- -	0
I	- -	1
L	- -	50
I	- -	1
I	- -	1
D	- -	500
E	- -	0
I	- -	1
		666

Chap. XIV. defcribes the true church and the progrefs of the reformation by the publifhing or *the everlafting gofpel*, which is fucceeded by an awful picture of the deftruction of antichrift.

Chap. XV. contains a vifion preparatory to feven angels pouring out the feven laft vials (cups or cenfers) of the wrath of God.

Chap. XVI. The vials are poured out, and effect the final deftruction of antichrift.

C   Chap.

Chap. XVII. reprefents the church of Rome under the emblem of a gaudy harlot, riding on the feven headed beaft. That this means Rome, befide the authorities cited by commentators, take the following from *Ganganelli*, afterwards Pope Clement XIV.

Inviting the Abbé Ferghen to vifit Rome, he tells him that it " may be feen a thoufand times and always with new pleafure. This city, fituated upon SEVEN HILLS, which the ancients call the feven miftreffes of the world, feems to command the univerfe, and boldly to fay to mankind, that fhe is the QUEEN and the CHIEF." *Letter* II. Englifh edition.

Chap. XVIII. defcribes the utter deftruction of fpiritual Babylon.

Chap. XIX. the triumph of the church thereon.

Chap. XX. reprefents the millenial ftate, or a thoufand years of the churches glory; and a fhort period of dreadful calamity between that and the day of judgment.

Chap. XXI, XXII. The new heaven, the new earth, and the new Jerufalem; differently underftood either of the millenium or of heaven itfelf. This leads to the conclufion.

Having thus given the reader a very brief fketch of the plan and contents of the Apocalypfe, we fhall introduce him to the following authors in the order in which they wrote; forbearing our further obfervations till the reader has gone through them.

No. I.

No. I. ARCHBISHOP BROWN, A. D. 1551.

Dr. George Brown, Abp. of Dublin, (confecrated by Abp. Cranmer) was a man of confiderable piety and learning, the firft proteftant bifhop in Ireland, and very inftrumental in the reformation of that kingdom.

Within a dozen years of the foundation of the order of Jesuits, he preached a fermon at Chrift Church, Dublin, (the year abovementioned) in which he gave the following character of that order.

" There is a *new* fraternity of late fprung up, who call themfelves *Jefuits*, which will *deceive* many, who are much after the fcribes and pharifees manner: amongft the Jews they fhall ftrive to abolifh the truth, and fhall come very near to do it; for thefe forts will turn themfelves into feveral forms, with the heathen an heathenift, with atheifts an atheift, with Jews a Jew, and with the reformers a reformade, purpofely to know your intentions, your minds, your hearts, and your inclinations; and thereby bring you at laft to be like the *fool* that *faid in his heart, there is no God*. Thefe fhall fpread over the whole *world*, fhall be admitted into the *councils* of *princes* and they never the wifer; charming of them; yea, making your princes reveal their hearts, and the fecrets therein unto them, and yet they not perceive it; which will happen from failing from the law of God....and by winking at their fins; yet in the end, God, to juftify his law, fhal fuddenly cut off this fociety, even *by the hands of thofe who have moft fuccoured them*, and made ufe of them; fo that at the end they fhall become *odious*

C 2

to all nations: they fhall be worfe than Jews having no refting place upon earth, and then fhall a Jew have more favour than a Jefuit." [HARLEIAN MISCELLANY, vol. V. p. 566.]

It need not be added, that this character proved prophetic. It fhall only be noted that this order, which was founded by *Ignatius Loyola* in 1540, was expelled England in 1604.---Venice, 1606---Portugal, 1759---France, 1764---Spain and Sicily, 1767---and totally fuppreffed by Pope Clement XIV. 1773.

No. II. REV. JOHN KNOX, 1572.

THIS intrepid Scots reformer, " who never feared the face of man," is faid, in feveral inftances, to have been indowed with a prophetic fpirit. The like has been afferted of *Luther*, *Hufs*, *Wifhart*, *Ufher*, and other eminent characters, of which the reader will form his own judgment. The following, at this period, muft ftrike many, as correfponding at once with recent events, and with that awful declaration of heaven, that God " vifiteth the fins of the fathers upon the children, unto the third and fourth generation."

The news of the horrid Maffacre of Paris was brought to Edinburgh about the twelfth of September, by Mr. *Killegrew*, ambaffador from Queen *Elizabeth*. Mr. Knox, introduced it into his next fermon, with his ufual denunciation of God's vengeance thereon, which he defired the French ambaffador, Monf. *Le Croque*, might be acquainted with.

with. The denunciation was to this purport, "Sentence is pronounced in Scotland againft that murderer, the *King* of *France*, and God's vengeance fhall never depart from him, nor his houfe, but his name fhall remain an *execration* to pofterity; and *none that fhall come of his loins* fhall enjoy that kingdom in peace and quietnefs, unlefs repentance prevent God's judgement." The Ambaffador, being told it, applied to the Regent and Council, and complained that his mafter was called a *traitor* and *murderer* of his fubjects under a promife and truft; and defired that an edict might be publifhed, prohibiting the fubjects of Scotland to fpeak any thing to the difhonour of his mafter; efpecially the Minifters in their fermons. This was waved by the Council; and the Ambaffador was told, that they could not hinder the Minifters from fpeaking even againft themfelves. [LIFE of KNOX.]

───────────

No. III. DR. THOMAS GOODWIN, 1639.

THIS excellent and venerable divine, who was fometime prefident of Magdalen college, Oxford, and one of the ejected minifters, wrote his Expofition of the Revelation in 1639, and it was publifhed in the year 1683, foon after his death.

On Rev. xi. 13. this writer obferves, "By the tenth part of the city I underftand fome one tenth part of Europe;" which he afterwards explains of the kingdom of France, as we fhall fee prefently. He goes on to obferve

"By

" By the earthquake here is meant a great concuſſion or ſhaking of ſtates, politic, or eccle-ſiaſtical...By this earthquake's falling thus out in a tenth part of the city, this tenth part of it is ſo ſhaken that it *falls*; that is, ceaſeth to be a tenth part of the city, or belong to its juriſdiction any longer...The effect of this earthquake, and fall of this tenth part of the city, is killing *ſeven thouſand of the names of men*....Now, by men of name, in ſcripture is meant men of title, office and dignity...[As in the caſe of Corah's conſpiracy,] ſo here a civil puniſhment falls upon theſe: for having killed theſe witneſſes, themſelves are to be killed (haply) by being BEREFT OF THEIR NAMES AND TITLES, which are to be *rooted out for ever*, and condemned to perpetual forgetfulneſs."

" Now which of theſe ten kingdoms [may be intended]....it is not hard to conjecture; though it be raſhneſs peremtorily to determine."...

" The ſaints and churches of *France*, God has made a wonder unto me in all his proceedings to-wards them, firſt and laſt; and there would ſeem ſome great and ſpecial honour reſerved for them, yet at the laſt; for it is certain, that the firſt light of the goſpel, by that firſt and ſecond angel's preach-ing in chapter xiv. (which laid the foundation of antichriſt's ruin) was out from among them, namely thoſe of Lyons, and other places in France. And they bore and underwent the great heat of that morning of perſecution, which was as great, if not greater than any ſince...And ſo, as that kingdom had the *firſt* great ſtroke, ſo now it ſhould have the honour of having the *laſt* great ſtroke in the ruin of Rome."

It ſhould be added, however, that Dr. Goodwin was ſo far from being poſitive in this idea, that he

rather

rather inclined to think Great Britain the tenth part of the city intended by the Holy Spirit; and that these great events should happen about the middle of the seventeenth century; in this last idea, however he lived to find himself mistaken, not dying till the year 1679.

No. IV. REV. CHRISTOPHER LOVE, 1651.

Mr. Love, a pious Presbyterian minister, who was beheaded during the troublesome times of the civil wars in this country, on a charge of conspiring with some others to restore K. Charles I. on the hope of his having been reformed and converted, after he had taken the Scotch covenant. This gentleman, who must be confessed a little tinctured with enthusiasm, had studied the Revelation, and was very confident in his calculation, in which he thought himself guided " by the Holy Spirit of the Lord."

The following prophecy, as it is called, is partly the result of his prophetic speculations, and partly his interpretation of a supposed pillar of Seth in Damascus, which it is now generally agreed by the learned was a gross imposition on the credulity of former ages. The *near* approach to late events in some of the following articles, is however sufficiently remarkable to interest attention in the present situation of affairs. The work from which the ensuing extract is taken is called, *A short Work of the Lord in the latter Age of the World.*

" Great earthquakes and commotions by sea and

and land fhall come in the year of God 1779.---
GREAT WARS in Germany and in AMERICA in
1780.---The deftruction of popery, or BABYLON'S
FALL, in the year 1790---God will be known by
many in the year 1795. This will produce a great
man---The ftars will wander, and the moon turn
as blood, in 1800---Africa, Afia, and America will
tremble in 1803---A great earthquake over all the
world, in 1805---God will be univerfally known by
all: then a general reformation, and peace for ever,
when the people fhall learn war no more---Happy
is the man that liveth to fee this day!"

A copy of this prophecy (with fome obvious
but material errors in the latter dates) may be
found in Mr. TOPLADY'S Pofthumous Works,
there faid to be communicated to him by the late
Dr. GIFFORD, one of the librarians of the Britifh
Mufeum.

No. V. ARCHBISHOP USHER. 1655.

THIS truly great man, equally eminent for his fingular learning and uncommon piety, is faid to have
been in feveral inftances endowed with a prophetic
fpirit, by which he foretold the Irifh maffacre forty
years before it came to pafs, in a fermon preached
in Dublin in 1601, where, from Ezek. iv. 6. dif-
courfing concerning the prophet's bearing the iniquity of Judah forty days, the Lord therein ap-
pointed a day for a year; he made this direct application in relation to the government's conni-
vance at popery at that time. " From this year
(fays

(fays he) will I reckon the fin of Ireland, that thofe *whom you now embrace,* fhall be your ruin, and *you* fhall bear this iniquity." Which prediction proved exactly true; for from that time 1601, to the year 1641, was juft forty years, in which it is notorious that the rebellion and maffacre in Ireland happened, which was accomplifhed by thofe popifh priefts and other papifts, who were then connived at and encouraged.

Of this fermon the bifhop referved the notes, and put a note thereof in the margin of his Bible; and the nearer the time was, the more confident he grew, that it was near accomplifhment, though there was no vifible appearance of any fuch thing; and (fays Dr. Bernard, his chaplain) "The year before the rebellion broke forth, the bifhop taking his leave of me, being then going from Ireland to England, he advifed me to a ferious preparation, for I fhould fee *heavy forrows and miferies* before I faw him again;" which he delivered with as great confidence, as if he had feen it with his eyes; which feems to verify that of the prophet, Amos iii. 7. " Surely the Lord will do nothing, but he will reveal it to his fervants the prophets."

By the fame fpirit of prophecy, and from the encouragement given by government to papifts, he forefaw the changes and miferies coming on England, both in church and ftate; and in particular the *death* of K. Charles I. of whom he would be often fpeaking with fear and trembling, even when he had the greateft fuccefs, and would therefore conftantly pray, and gave all advice poffible to prevent any fuch thing.

Laftly, he predicted that " the *greateft ftroke upon the reformed churches was yet to come;*—and that the time of the utter ruin of the fee of Rome, *fhould*

D   *be*

be when fhe thought herfelf moft fecure:" and as to
this laft, we fhall add a brief account from the per-
fon's own hand, to whom he related it the year before he died.

" I prefumed to inquire of him, what his prefent apprehenfions were concerning a very *great
perfecution* which fhould fall upon the church of
God in thefe nations of England, Scotland, and
Ireland, of which this reverend primate had fpoken
with great confidence many years before, when we
were in the higheft and fulleft ftate of outward
peace and fettlement. I alfo afked him, " Whether he did believe thofe fad times to be paft, or
that they were yet to come." To which he an-
fwered, " That they were yet to come; and that
he did as confidently expect it as ever he had done:"
Adding, " That this fad perfecution would fall
upon *all the Proteftant churches in Europe."* I re-
plied, " That I did hope it might have been paft
as to thefe nations of ours, fince I thought, that
though we, who are the people thereof, have been
punifhed much lefs than our fins have deferved,
and that our late wars had made far lefs devaftations
than war commonly does upon thofe countries.
where it pleafeth God in judgment to fuffer them;
yet we muft needs acknowledge, that many great
houfes have been burnt, ruined, and left without
inhabitants, many great families impoverifhed and
undone, and many lives alfo had been loft in that
bloody war, and that Ireland and Scotland, as well
as England, had drank very deep of the *cup of God's
anger,* even to the overthrow of the government,
and the utter defolation, almoft of a very great part
of thofe countries."

But this holy man turning to me, and fixing
his eyes upon me, with a ferious and ireful look,

which

which he ufually had when he fpake God's word,
and not his own, and when the power of God
feemed to be upon him, and to conftrain him to
fpeak, which I could eafily difcern much to differ
from the countenance wherewith he ufually *fpake to
me*; he faid thus:

" Fool not yourfelf with fuch hopes, for I tell
you, all you have yet feen hath been but the beginning of forrows, to what is yet *to come upon the
Proteftant churches of Chrift*, who will *ere long fall
under a fharper perfecution than ever yet was upon
them*: and therefore (faid he to me) *look you be not
found in the outward court, but a worfhipper in the
temple before the altar*; *for Chrift will meafure all
thofe that profefs his name, and call themfelves his
people*; and the outward worfhippers he *will leave
out* to be *trodden down* by the Gentiles. The out-
ward court (fays he) is the *formal Chriftian*, whofe
religion lies in performing the outward duties of
chriftianity, without having an *inward life and
power of faith uniting them to Chrift*, and thefe God
will leave to be trodden down, and fwept away by
the Gentiles; but the worfhippers *within the temple*, and *before the altar*, are thofe who do *indeed*
worfhip God *in fpirit and in truth*, whofe *fouls* are
made his temple, and he is honoured and adored in
the *moft inward thoughts* of their hearts, and they
facrifice their lufts and vile affections, yea, and
their *own wills* to him; and thefe God will hide in
the *hollow of his hand*, and *under the fhadow of his
wings*. And this fhall be one great difference between *this laft*, and all the other preceding perfecutions: for in the *former* the moft *eminent* and *fpiritual minifters and Chriftians* did generally fuffer
moft, and were moft violently fallen upon; but in
this *laft perfecution* thefe fhall be preferved by God,

as a feed to partake of that glory which shall *immediately follow*, and come upon the church, as soon as ever this storm shall be over; for as it shall be the *sharpest*, so it shall be the *shortest perfecution of them all*; and shall only take away the *grofs hypocrites* and *formal profeffors*, but the true spiritual believers shall be preserved till the calamity be over."

He added, " That the Papists were, in his opinion, the Gentiles spoken of in the 11th of the Revelations, to whom the *outward court should be left*, that they might tread it under foot: they having received the Gentiles' worship, in their adoring images, and saints departed, and in taking to themselves many mediators: and this (said he) the Papists are now designing among themselves, and therefore be sure you may be ready."

This was the substance, and I think (for the greatest part) the very same words which this holy man spake to me at the time before mentioned, not long before his death, and which he writ down, that so great and notable a prediction might not be loft and forgotten by myself and others.

" This gracious man repeated the same things in substance to his only daughter the lady Tyrril, and that with many tears, and much about the same time....The same things he also repeated to the lady Byffe, wife to the present lord chief baron of Ireland, but with adding this circumstance, That *if they brought back the king it might be delayed a little longer:* but (saith he) it will surely come, therefore be sure to look that you be not found unprepared for it.

To conclude in the words of Dr. Bernard: speaking of this excellent person, he says, " Howfoever I am as far from heeding of prophecies this
way

way as any; yet with me it is not improbable, that so great a divine, so sanctified from his youth, so knowing and eminent throughout the universal church; might have, at some special times, more than ordinary motions and impulses, in doing the watchman's part, of giving warning of judgments shortly to happen."

No. VI. Dr. H. MORE, 1663.

THIS learned writer has taken considerable pains to develope the depths of the "MYSTERY *of* INIQUITY contained in the kingdom of *Antichrist*." On that remarkable prediction, Revelation xi. 13. he observes, [Book II. ch. 12.]

"That an *earthquake* signifies political commotions and change of affairs, is obvious to any one to note; but that the *City* here mentioned should be understood not of a city of brick or stone, but a *Polity*, has not been so easy for every one to hit on; but I conceive it is plain enough that this city is the very city mentioned in the eighth verse, which is called the great *city*, and this great city is the whore of Babylon; and the whore of Babylon is nothing but the body of the idolatrous clergy in the empire, who appertain to the seventh or last head of the beast, which is an head of blasphemy, as well as the six first, that is to say, of idolatrous head. Whence we may understand what is meant by these *seven thousand names of men*; for neither seven nor thousand signify any determinate number, but only the nature or property of these *names of*

men

men that are faid to be flain, namely, that they are TITLES, DIGNITIES, OFFICES or ORDERS of men belonging to the ftate of Chriftendom. As under the feventh head, that is become idolatrous and antichriftian, and in that this number *feven* is multiplied into a *thoufand*, it fignifies a perfect and. durable *nulling* all fuch *offices* and ORDERS of men; which, if Mr. *Mede* had taken notice of, it would have faved him the labour of making out the fenfe of *names of men*, and alfo the folicitude touching the proportionablenefs of the number of the flain; for no men at all here are *neceffarily* implied to be flain, but only all antichriftian OFFICES and FRATERNITIES to be DISSOLVED and ABROGATED, and things to be reduced to the purity of the firft four hundred years. For to *flay*, by a diorifmus, fignifies nothing elfe but a caufing a thing to *ceafe to be*. This, but little queftion, is the true meaning of this place. And the *tenth part of the city* will have a fenfe *marvellous coincident* therewith.

No. VII.   REV. PETER JURIEU, 1687.

MR. JURIEU was one of the Minifters of the French church at Rotterdam, and is famous for a work, entitled, " *The* ACCOMPLISHMENT *of the* SCRIPTURE PROPHECIES; or the *approaching deliverance* of the church"---Originally written in French; but a tranflation was printed in this country, of the above date, from which are taken the following extracts.

This work, the author (in his *prefatory* addrefs) profeffes

profeffes to have been the fruit of much prayer, and ftudy of the fcriptures, in the fearch of which he is confident of having received an anfwer to his prayers in the way of divine illumination, infomuch that he fays, (part II. p. 68) " We fhall fee fuch an *admirable agreement* between the events and the prophecies explained, that fhall abundantly convince, that what I am about to fay, is *not* SIMPLE *conjecture*."

On Revel. xi. 13. the author defcants thus: (p. 242 and fequel.)---" There fhall be an *earthquake*, *i. e.* a great emotion and trouble in the world, and in the antichriftian kingdom. In this emotion a *tenth part of the city* fhall *fall*; *i. e.* a tenth part of the antichriftian kingdom fhall be taken away from it. *Seven thoufand men* fhall perifh in this earthquake, and be buried under the ruins of the city, *i. e.* that this fhall be brought about with fome bloodfhed (though not confiderable) in that part of the city which fhall be taken away from the Pope and the Popedom. And laftly, within a little while this tenth part of the city which fhall be taken from the Popedom, fhall give glory to God, and be converted."

After a few pages it is added—" Mark that the great earthquake, *i. e.* the great alteration of affairs in the land of the papacy, muft for *that time* happen only in the *tenth part* of the city that fhall *fall*: for this fhall be the effect of this earthquake."

" Now what is this *tenth part of the city*, which fhall *fall?* In my opinion, we cannot doubt that 'tis FRANCE. This kingdom is the moft confiderable *part* or piece of the ten horns, or ftates, which once made up the great *Babylonian city*: it *fell*; this does not fignify, that the *French Monarchy* fhall

fhall be *ruined*; it may be HUMBLED; but in all appearance, Providence does defign a great elevation for her afterward. 'Tis highly probable that God will not let go unpunifhed the horrible outrages which it acts at this day [of perfecution] Afterward, it muft build its greatnefs upon the ruins of the *papal empire*, and enrich itfelf with the fpoils of thofe who fhall take part with the *papacy*. They who...*perfecute* the *proteftants*, know not whither God is leading them: this is not the way by which he will lead *France* to the height of glory. If fhe comes thither, 'tis becaufe fhe fhall fhortly change her road. Her greatening will be no damage to *proteftant ftates*; on the contrary, the *proteftant ftates* fhall be enriched with the fpoils of others; and be ftrengthened by the *fall of Antichrift's empire*. This *tenth* part of the *city* fhall *fall*, with refpect to the *papacy*; it fhall break with *Rome*, and the *Roman religion*. One thing is certain, that the *Babylonian empire* fhall perifh through the refufal of obedience by the *ten kings*, who had given their power to the *beaft*. The thing is already come to pafs in part. The kingdoms of Sweden, Denmark, England, and feveral fovereign ftates in Germany, have withdrawn themfelves from the jurifdiction of the pope. *They have fpoiled the harlot* of her riches. *They have eaten her flefh*, i. e. feized on her *benefices*, and *revenues*, which fhe had in their countries. This muft go on, and be finifhed as it is begun. The kings who yet remain under the empire of Rome, muft break with her, leave her folitary and defolate.

" But who muft begin this *laft revolt*? It is moft probable that FRANCE fhall. Not Spain, which as yet is plunged in *fuperftition*, and is as much under the *tyranny* of the *clergy* as ever. Not the emperor,

peror, who in *temporals* is fubject to the pope, and permits that in his ftates the archbifhop of Strigonium fhould teach, that the pope can *take* away the Imperial crown from him. It cannot be any country but *France*, which a long time ago hath begun to *fhake off the yoke of Rome*. It is well known, how folemnly and openly war hath been declared againft the pope, by a declaration of the king (ratified in all the parliaments) by the *decifions* of the affembly of the French clergy, by a *difputaticn* againft the authority of the pope, managed in the Sorbon, folemnly and by order of the court. And to heighten the affront, the *thefes* were pofted up, even upon the gates of his Nuncio. Nothing of this kind had hitherto happened, at leaft in a time of peace, and unlefs the pope had given occafion by his infolence.

" Befides this, *fuperftition* and *idolatry* lofe their credit much in *France*.—There is a fecret party, though well enough known, which greatly defpifeth the popular devotions, images, worfhip of faints, and is convinced that thefe are human inventions. God is before-hand preparing for this great work.

" To this it may be objected, that for the laft hundred and fifty years, the pope's empire hath not been made up of ten kings, becaufe the kings of England, Sweden, Denmark, &c. have thrown off his government; and confequently, France is not at this day the *tenth* part of the Babylonian empire ; for it is *more* than a *tenth* part of it. But this is no difficulty : for we muft know, that things retain the *names* which they bore in their original (without regarding the alterations which time does bring along. Though at this day, there are not ten kingdoms under the Babylonian empire, it is notwithftanding certain, that each kingdom was called, and ought

E   to

to be called in this prophecy, the *tenth* part, becaufe the prophet having defcribed this empire in
its beginning, by its *ten horns*, or *ten kings*, it is
necessary for our clear underftanding, that every
one of thefe *ten* kings and kingdoms fhould' be
called *one* of the *ten kings*, or of the *ten kingdoms*,
with refpect to the original conftitution of the antichriftian empire.

" Seeing the *tenth part* of the *city* that muft *fall*, is
France, this gives me fome hopes that the *death* of
the *two witneffes* hath a particular relation to *this
kingdom*. It is the *ftreet* or place of *this city*, i. e.
the moft fair and eminent part of it. The *witneffes*
muft remain dead upon *this ftreet*, and upon it they
muft be raifed again. And as the *death* of the *witneffes* and their refurrection have a relation to the
kingdom of France, it may well fall out, that we may
not be far diftant from the *time* of the *refurrection* of
the *witneffes*, feeing the three years and a half of
their *death* are either begun, or will begin fhortly.

" *And in the earthquake were flain feven thoufand*;
in the Greek it is, *feven thoufand names of men*, and
not feven thoufand *men*. I confefs, that this feems
fomewhat myfterious: in other places we find not
this phrafe, *names of men*, put fimply for *men*. Perhaps there is here a figure of grammar called, *hy-
pallage cafus*, fo that *names of men* are put for *men of
name*, i. e. of raifed and confiderable quality, be it
on the account of riches, or of dignity, or of learning. But I am more inclined to fay, that here
thefe words, *names of men*, muft be taken in their
natural fignification, and do intimate, that the *total
reformation of France* fhall *not* be made with bloodfhed, nothing fhall be deftroyed but NAMES; fuch
as are the names of Monks, of Carmelites, of Au-
guftines, of Dominicans, of Jacobins, of Francif-
                                                    cans,

cans, Capuchins, Jefuits, Minimes, and an infinite
company. of others, whofe number it is not eafy to
define, and which the Holy Ghoft denotes by the
number *feven*, which is the number of perfection,
to fignify, that the orders of monks and nuns fhall
perifh for ever.   This is an inftitution fo degene-
rated from its firft original, that it is become the
arm of antichrift.   Thefe orders cannot perifh one
without another.

   " Thefe great 'events deferve to be. diftinguifhed
from all others; for they have changed, or fhall
change, THE WHOLE FACE OF THE WORLD."

   In page 270 we find thefe words :—" 'Tis clear,
that thefe *kings* who through ignorance, or weak-
nefs, fuffered *their power* to be ufurped by the *empire* of the *papacy*, fhall take it again; *fhall eat her
flefh i. e.* fhall enrich themfelves with her benefices,
and revenues, *and burn her with fire*, i. e. fhall
abolifh the *memory* of this *Romifh empire*, fo that nothing but afhes fhall remain of it."

   And again he fays, in page 276, " The firft
thing, which fhall be done in the *third* period of
the *feventh* vial, is the *fall* of the *tenth* part of the
city, i. e. of *the kingdom of France*, which fhall break
with the *court of Rome*, and wholly change the face
of *religion* in that *kingdom*, this is the firft action of
the *vintage.*

   " The *beaft* and the falfe *prophet*, the *Pope* and
his *agents* fhall *rally* all their *forces:* but God fhall
mufter all his together, and give the laft blow to
popery: then the beaft and the falfe *prophet* fhall
be thrown into the lake, and plunged into the bottomlefs pit: *Babylon* fhall wholly *fall*; and it fhall
be faid, fhe *is fallen*, fhe is fallen."

   After fome further obfervations, he goes on,
in page 260 :—" *And after*; thefe words fignify,
         E 2   that

that when the *reformation* fhall be eflaftblifhed again
in *France*, by way of divine immediate operation,
by which the zeal of the apoftates, and of others
who know the truth, but with-hold it in unrigh-
teoufnefs, fhall be quickened again; fome fpace of
time fhall pafs, probably fome *years* before *France*
fhall wholly throw off the *yoke of Popery*. That·
kingdom fhall not be intirely *reformed* by way of authority, immediately after our reformation fhall be
again fet on foot by way of infpiration, and reco-
vering of zeal. For, *and after*, fignifies an interval
of time; but whether it fhall be fhort, or long,
is not expreffed: notwithftanding, I fee no likeli-
hood, that it fhall be very long, nor do I believe
fo."

Mentioning the time in which he expected thefe
events, this author fays, [Part II. page 50.] " That
it will fall on the year 1785, in which fhall come
the glorious reign of Jefus Chrift on the earth of
which we fhall fpeak afterwards."

Again in page 279, he goes on thus:—" If I
fhould be miftaken *nine* or *ten years*,—I do not
think that any could juftly treat me as a falfe prophet, and accufe me of rafhnefs. Many will not
forbear to judge me *rafh*, becaufe I propound my
conjectures about thefe things as certain conclu-
fions. To this I have a *fecond* thing to fay, that
none hath reafon to be offended, that I am *poffef-
fed* with, and *perfuaded* of that, which I think
I evidently fee, and that I find the proofs of what
I propound convincing to myfelf, I fhould do ill
to demand of others the fame affurance, and oblige
them to entertain the fame perfwafion; I declare
the contrary in exprefs terms: I am well content
(as I have faid) that my readers fhould account
thefe affertions to be conjectures, ·provided that I
                                                   may

may have the liberty to believe what I fee, or what I believe I fee in the *writings* of the *Prophets.*"

The author afterwards treating more fully of the introduction of Chrift's kingdoms, p. 376. places the order of events as follows. " 1. The papal empire fhall fall. 2. After that fome *years* will be neceffary to abolifh *fects* and *parties*, and compofe the differences among *Chriftians.* 3. That after this, many *Heathen nations*, and the *Jews* fhall be *converted:* for it cannot be thought, that they fhould be converted, while *Chriftians* are fo much at variance among themfelves, and feeking the deftruction of one another. 4. After the converfion of the *Jews*, the remainder of the moft remote *nations* fhall alfo be converted; now for all this there muft be time; for fhould we think that God will act in a more miraculous manner in *this*, than in the eftablifhment of the *firft* Chriftian church? Wherefore, as the *Chriftian church* was near an hundred *years* in its firft fettling, no lefs will be neceffary perfectly to refettle it; and *then* fhall that bleffed *kingdom* come, which we expect; not but there is fome probability, that God may begin to compute the *thoufand years* from the *fall* of *Antichrift*, even before the converfion of the *Jews* and *Gentiles*, and fo the *fall* of the *Antichriftian kingdom*, and the converfion of the *nations*, may in fome fort be comprehended within the *reign of Chrift for a thoufand years.* But when we fpeak here of the *kingdom of Chrift*, we fpeak of it as in its perfection, which will not be till after thefe things are come to pafs."

Among the characters of Chrift's reign the following are the moft ftriking, page 378:—" The *fourth* character of this reign of Chrift, is a *fovereign peace.* This is plainly revealed by many ex-

prefs

prefs prophecies. That *the wolf fhall feed with the lamb*, and *fwords be turned into plough-fhares*, and *men fhall not hurt or deftroy one another*. The art of war which fprung from *hell*, fhall return *thither*. Nothing but the corruption and wickednefs of the world doth make it neceffary. The Devil of Covetoufnefs, and of Ambition, the fpirit of Revenge, and the like, fhall return to the bottomlefs pit, whence they came. And it fhall no more be a point of honour to know how to maffacre mankind, to ftorm towns and gain battles, and deftroy countries, and cover the fields with dead bodies."

Then follows his fifth character, in thefe words, fo very remarkable, when we confider what has lately taken place in France, with refpect to titles, armorial bearings, and liveries, &c.— " This fhall be *a kingdom of humility*. All thofe VAIN TITLES, which now ferve for ornament and pride, fhall then be vanquifhed. *Brotherly love* fhall make all men *equal*; not that all diftinction, and all dignities among men fhall ceafe. This *kingdom* is no *anarchy*; there fhall be fome to govern, and to obey. But government fhall then be without pride and infolence, without tyranny, and without violence. Subjects fhall obey their rulers, with an humble fpirit; and governors fhall rule their fubjects, with a fpirit of meeknefs and gentlenefs."

No.

No. VIII. REV. ROBERT FLEMING. 1701.

M<small>R</small>. F<small>LEMING</small>, Minifter of the Scots church in London, publifhed fome extraordinary D<small>ISCOURSES</small>, and one in particular of the above date, on the R<small>ISE</small> and F<small>ALL</small> of the P<small>APACY</small>, from which the following extracts are taken.

" The fourth vial comes now to be confidered. And as this is poured out *upon the fun of the papal kingdom*, ver. 8 ; fo the effect of it is *men's being fcorched or burned with fire*, which yet does not make them turn to God, but blafpheme his name the more, as we may fee, ver. 9. Now as this vial muft begin where the other ends, viz. at, or a little after the year 1648 ; fo I cannot fee but it muft denote the wars that followed the peace of Munfter, with other incidental occurences....Now feeing the bombarding of towns and cities was chiefly made ufe of in thefe latter wars, we may fee how properly *the fcorching or burning men from above* (as if the *fun* had fent down fire and heat from his own body) is made ufe of to characterize the time of this vial. But the chief thing to be taken notice of here, is, that the *fun* and other luminaries of heaven, are the emblem of princes and kingdoms, as we took notice before. Therefore the pouring out this vial on the *fun*, muft denote the *humiliation* of fome eminent potentates of the Romifh intereft, whofe influences and countenance cherifh and fupport the papal caufe. And thefe therefore muft be principally underftood of the *houfes* of *Auftria* and *Bourbon*, though not exclufively of other popifh princes....

" And now, feeing I have marked out the time
we

we are in at prefent, it is time alfo to put a ftop to
our Apocalyptical thoughts; feeing no man can
pretend, upon any juft grounds, to calculate future
times.   However, feeing I have come fo far, I
fhall adventure to prefent you further with fome
conjectural thoughts on this head; for I am far
from the prefumption of fome men, to give them
any higher character.

"Now my conjectures fhall relate to two things,
viz. to the remaining part of this vial, and to the
other vials that follow this.

"And, 1. as to the remaining part of this vial,
I do humbly fuppofe that it will come to its higheft
pitch about An. 1717, and that it will run out about
the year 1794...So that there is ground to hope, that
about the beginning of another fuch century, things
may again alter for the better : for I cannot but hope
that fome new mortification of the chief fupporters
of antichrift will then happen; and perhaps the
French monarchy may begin to be confiderably
humbled about that time : that whereas the prefent
French king takes the *fun* for his emblem, and this
for his motto, *Nec pluribus impar*, he may at length,
or rather his fucceffors, and the Monarchy itfelf (at
leaft before the year 1794) be forced to acknowledge, that in refpect to neighbouring potentates,
he is even *fingulis impar*.

"But as to the expiration of this vial, I do fear it
will not be until the year 1794.) The reafon of
which conjecture is this; that I find the pope got
a new foundation of exaltation, when Juftinian, upon
his conqueft of Italy, left it in a great meafure to
the pope's management, being willing to eclipfe
his own authority, to advance that of this haughty
prelate.   Now this being in the year 552; this, by
the addition of the 1260 years, reaches down to
the

the year 1811; which, according to prophetical account is the year 1794.

"And now, my friends, I may be well excufed; if I venture no further, in giving you any more conjectural thoughts upon this prefent periód of time. But feeing I pretend to give my fpeculations of what is future, no higher character than gueffes, I fhall ftill venture to add fomething to what I have already faid. Therefore be pleafed; 1. To call to mind, what I premifed to the confideration of the feven vials, as the fecond preliminary, viz. " that feeing the vials do (all of them) fuppofe a ftruggle or war between the *popifh* and *reformed* parties; every vial is to be looked upon, as the event and conclufion of fome new periodical attack of that firft party upon this other; the iffue of which proves at length favourable to the latter againft the former." For if this be duly confidered, it will let us fee, that *great declining* of the *Proteftant intereft* for fome time, and *great and formidable advances*, and *new degrees of increafe* in the *Romifh party*, are very confiftent with the ftate of both thefe oppofite interefts under the vials. For, as Rome Pagan was gradually ruined under the feals, under many of which it feemed to increafe to outward obfervation, and to become more rampant than before, when yet it was indeed declining; fo muft we fuppofe it will be with Rome Papal. For monarchies as they rife gradually and infenfibly, fo do they wear out fo likewife. And therefore we muft not entertain fuch chimerical notions of the *fall* of the papacy, as if it were to be accomplifhed fpeedily or miraculoufly, as many have done. For as it rofe infenfibly, and ftep by ftep, fo muft it fall in like manner. . . .

" And as a confirmation of this conjecture, let

F   it

it be confidered in the fecond place (befides what I
hinted before on this head) that it is fomething
very extraordinary, and peculiar in fome fenfe to
this vial, *that the fun, upon which it is poured out,
fhould yet be made the executor of the judgment of it
upon others, at the fame time that he is tormented with
it himfelf.* So that whofoever is denoted by the *fun*
here (as I fuppofe *the Houfe of Bourbon* principally
is) is made ufe of, as the Devil is, both to torment
others, and to be tormented himfelf in fo doing.
And if the *King of France* therefore be denoted by
this principally, I fear he is yet to be made ufe of,
in the hand of God, as Nebuchadnezzar was of old
againft the Jews, viz. as a further fevere fcourge to
the proteftant churches every where. And, befides this charaɛteriftical mark, which feems to
forebode his further exaltation and our humiliation;
there is yet a third thing, that I cannot but think
upon with dread and trembling of heart, viz. that it
is further faid, " that while this fun of the *popifh*
world is running his fatal and dreadful career, and
fcorching men with fire, they are fo far from being
bettered by thefe judgments, that they go on more
and more to blafpheme the name of God, who has
power over thefe plagues. And while this con-
tinues to be the ftate of the proteftant world, and
while atheifm, deifm, focinianifm, irreligion, pro-
fanenefs, fcepticifm, formality, hatred of godlinefs,
and a bitter perfecuting fpirit, continue and increafe
among us, what can we expeɛt but new and defo-
lating judgments? . . .

　　"If any fay, that thefe are melancholy conjeɛtures,
I muft tell them that I cannot help the matter; for
I muft follow the thread of the text and the afpeɛt
of the times. If they afk, but when will the tide
turn for the proteftant church? I anfwer, when
　　　　　　　　　　　　　　　　　　　　　　they

they turn more univerſally to God, and no ſooner. But if they inquire further, whether the *ſun* of the *popiſh kingdom* is not to be *eclipſed* himſelf at length? I muſt poſitively aſſert he will; elſe this vial were not a judgment upon him and the Romiſh party. But if yet again the queſtion be, when this is to fall out and how? I muſt tell you, that I have nothing further to add to what I have ſaid, as to the time. But as to the manner, how this is to be done, our text does lay a foundation of ſome more diſtinct thoughts. Therefore, in the fourth and laſt place, we may juſtly ſuppoſe, that the *French monarchy,* after it has *ſcorched* others, will itſelf conſume by doing ſo; it's fire, and that which is the fuel that maintains it, waſting inſenſibly; till it be exhauſted at laſt towards the end of this century. . . .

" One thing only I ſhall further take notice of here, upon the occaſion of the king of Spain's death; that God ſeems to mark out great things ſometimes by very minute ones, ſuch as names, *e. g.* as the Spaniſh monarchy began with Charles the Fifth, (as to the Auſtrian family) ſo it has now expired in one of the ſame name: which I the rather obſerve, becauſe of many inſtances of the ſame kind. Of which number take theſe following: Darius the Mede, as Daniel calls him (though Xenophon calls him Cyaxares) the uncle of Cyrus, was the firſt Medo-Perſian monarch, after the deſtruction of the Babylonian; and Darius Codomannus was the laſt. Ptolemeus Lagi began the Egyptian kingdom after Alexander's death, and Ptolemeus Dionyſius was the laſt of that race. Auguſtus fixed the Roman empire, and it ended in Auguſtulus. The Eaſtern Roman empire was erected by Conſtantine the Great, and expired with Conſtantine Paleologus. The Scots race came into Eng-

land

land in a James, and has gone out again in another of that name. And whether William, the third king of England of that name, as well as the third William Prince of Orange, be likely to be the laft both thefe ways, is left to future time to unriddle.

"But 2. to proceed with my other conjectures relating to the remaining vials : I do further fuppofe that

"The fifth vial, ver. 10, 11. which is to be *poured out on the feat of the beaft*, or the dominions that more immediately belong to, and depend upon the Roman fee ; that, I fay, this judgment will probably begin about the year 1794, and expire about A. C. 1848 ; fo that the duration of it upon this fuppofition, will be for the fpace of 54 years. For I do fuppofe, that feeing the Pope received the title of Supreme Bifhop no fooner than An. 606, he cannot be fuppofed to have any vial poured upon his feat immediately (fo as to ruin his authority fo fignally as this judgment muft be fuppofed to do) until the year 1848, which is the date of the 1260 years in prophetical account, when they are reckoned from An. 606. But yet we are not to imagine that this vial will *totally* deftroy the papacy (though it will exceedingly weaken it) for we find this ftill in being and alive, when the next vial is poured out.

"The fixth vial, ver. 12, &c. will be poured out upon the Mahometan Antichrift, as the former on the Papacy. And feeing the fixth trumpet brought the Turks from beyond Euphrates, from croffing which river they date their rife : this fixth vial dries up their waves, and exhaufts their power, as the means and way to prepare and difpofe the eaftern kings and kingdoms to renounce their heathenifh and Mahometan errors, in order to their receiving and embracing Chriftianity.

" For I think this is the native import of the text, and not that the Jews are to be underſtood under this denomination of *the kings of the Eaſt* ; which is ſuch an odd ſtraining of it to ſerve a turn, as I cannot admit of. Now ſeeing this vial is to deſtroy the Turks, we hear of *three unclean ſpirits like frogs or toads*, that were ſent out by Satan and the *remains* of the polity and church of Rome, called the Beaſt and the Falſe Prophet, in order to inſinuate upon the eaſtern nations, upon their deſerting Mahometiſm, to fall in with their idolatrous and ſpurious Chriſtianity, rather than with the true reformed doctrine. And theſe meſſengers ſhall be ſo ſucceſsful as to draw theſe eaſtern kings and their ſubjects, and with them the greateſt part of mankind, to take part with them. So that, by the aſſiſtance of theſe their agents and miſſionaries, they ſhall engage the whole world in ſome manner, to join with them in rooting out the ſaints. (And here in a parentheſis Chriſt gives a watchword to his ſervants to be upon their guard in this hour of trial, ver. 15.) But when the Pope has got himſelf at the head of this vaſt army, and has brought them to the place of battle, called Armageddon (i. e. the place where there will be a moſt diabolical, cunning and powerful conſpiracy againſt Chriſt's followers ; then immediately doth the ſeventh angel pour out his vial to their ruin and deſtruction.

" The ſeventh vial therefore being *poured out on the air*, ver. 17. brings down *thunder, lightning, hail*, and *ſtorms* ; which, together with a terrible *earthquake*, deſtroys all the *antichriſtian nations*, and particularly Rome, or *myſtical Babylon*. And as Chriſt concluded his ſufferings on the croſs with this voice, *It is finiſhed* ; ſo the church's ſufferings are concluded with a voice out of the *temple of heaven*,

heaven, and from the *throne of God and Chrift* there, faying, *It is done*. And therefore with this doth the bleffed Millenium of Chrift's fpiritual reign on earth begin ; of which, and what may be fuppofed to follow, we took fome notice above.

" Now feeing thefe two vials are, as it were, one continued, the firft running into the fecond, and the fecond completing the firft ; the one giving us an account of the beaft's preparations for warring againft the faints, and the other fhewing the event of the whole : there is no need to give you any conjectures about the conclufion of the fixth vial, or the beginning of the laft ; only you may ob-ferve, that the firft of thefe will probably take up moft of the time between 1848, and the year 2000 ; becaufe fuch long *meffages* and *intrigues* (befides the time fpent before in deftroying the Turkifh em-pire) and preparations for fo univerfal a war, muft needs take up a great many years ; whereas our bleffed Lord feems to tell us, that the deftruction of all thofe his enemies will be accomplifhed fpeedily, and in a little time, in comparifon of the other vial. Suppofing then that the Turkifh mo-narchy fhould be totally deftroyed between 1848, and 1900, we may juftly affign feventy or eighty years longer to the end of the fixth feal, and but twenty or thirty at moft to the laft. Now how great and remarkable this laft deftruction of the papal antichrift will be, we may guefs by that reprefent-ation of it, chap. xiv. 19, 20. where it is fet forth under the emblem and character *of the great wine-prefs of the wrath of God* (which can refer to nothing properly but the event of the feventh vial, as I might fhew at large had I time.) Now this *wine-prefs is faid to be trodden without the city*, (viz. of Jerufalem, or the church, feeing this is called the
City,

City, in fcripture ftyle, as Rome is called the *Great City*) *in Armageddon*, Rev. xvi. 16. which may bear allufion to *the Valley of Decifion*, Joel iii. 2, 12, 14. However the greatnefs of this flaughter appears in this, that the blood is reprefented to flow in fuch a current as to reach even to *the horfe bridles*, viz. of the fervants of God, employed in this execution : for without doubt this relates to what we have, ch. xix. 14. which I befeech you to compare with this. . . . And now to return to the reprefentation of this flaughter by the *wine-prefs of blood*, chap. xiv. 20. it is further faid of it, that it *flowed to the height of the horfe bridles, for the fpace or extent of* 1600 *furlongs*. So that Armageddon feems to be denoted here, in the extent of it, as the *field of battle*, which is now turned into a *field of blood*. Now what place can we imagine to be fo properly meant by this as the *territory of the fee of Rome in Italy*, which (as Mr. Jofeph Mede, who firft made this obfervation, fays) from the city of Rome to the furthermoft mouth of the river Po and the marfhes of Verona, is extended the fpace of 200 Italian miles, that is exactly 1600 furlongs ; the Italian mile confifting of eight furlongs. . . . .

" And now, my friends, I have fulfilled my promife to you, in giving you not only *a refolution* of the grand Apocalyptical queftion, *When the papacy began, and when we may fuppofe it will end :* but fome confiderable improvement of it, with refpect to the knowledge not only of times paft, but that particular period we are now under, together with conjectures (and fome of them I am fure new and uncommon) about *future time*. By all which I hope I have given the world fuch a *key* to unlock all the chambers of the book of the Revelation, as I hope I may venture to fay (if confidered and ufed impar

tially

tially, judiciously, and diligently) will be found to give some new light to us, in our mental journey through the mazes and turnings and dark passages thereof."

No. IX. REV. MR. JOHN WILLISON. 1742.

THIS good man was minister of the gospel at Dundee, and among several sermons he published under the title of " The BALM of GILEAD—with the *Glory* of the *Ministration* of the *Spirit*," &c. are two (the 11th and 12th) on John iii. 30. *He must increase*— in which is the following passage, which has been lately noticed as remarkable, though the sentiment may be probably borrowed from some of the preceding authors.

" Before antichrift's fall, one of the ten kingdoms which supported the beast shall undergo a marvellous Revolution, Rev. xi. 13. *The same hour there was a great earthquake, and the tenth part of the city fell.* By which *tenth part*, is to be understood one of the ten kingdoms into which the great city Romish Babylon was divided: (this many take to be the kingdom of *France*, it being the *tenth* and last of the kingdoms as to the time of its rise, and that which gave Rome denomination of the beast with ten horns,) and also it being the only one of the ten that was never conquered since its rise. However unlikely this and other prophesied events may appear at the time, yet the Almighty hand of the only wise God can soon bring them about when least expected."

No.

No. X. ANONYMOUS. 1747.

THE writer here referred to is the unknown author
of a remarkable " DISSERTATION on the 13th and
14th verſes of the XIth chapter of the Revelation or an Enquiry into the *true Object* of the
ſecond Woe.—With probable Reaſons for ſhewing
that *the Tenth Part of the City* is deſcriptive of
FRANCE; and that the *Earthquake* with which it is
threatened intends a REVOLUTION in that Kingdom." This pamphlet was printed for John Bird,
Black Fryars, without a date, but from a paſſage
in the cloſe of it was evidently written in 1747,
which the author calls " the current year."

The object of this tract was avowedly to en-
courage the Engliſh nation in a war with France,
in hopes that it might be a means to effect the grand
event which he deſcribes in the following ſtrik-
ing paſſages, which form the principal part of the
pamphlet.

" I. Concerning the true object of the SECOND
WOE.

" The ſecond woe appears to have a *double* object; namely,

" 1. The Roman papal empire at large. By
this means it involves all the wars affecting that
empire, both in the eaſtern and weſtern parts of it,
from the time that the Turks were let looſe upon
it, about A. D. 1321, to the laſt overthrow given
them by Prince Eugene, when he took Belgrade,
A. D. 1717; completing their period of 396
years; the *preciſe time* for which they are ſaid to be
looſed.....

" 2. The *other* remarkable object of the ſecond

G   woe,

woe, is exhibited to us under the character of the *tenth part of the city*; including the calamities which that branch of the papal hierarchy is to suffer, as an introduction to a *general reformation* in the church. . . . .

" Here then the only inquiry is : What is the particular state or kingdom pointed out to us by *the tenth part of the city?*—Authors are much divided in their sentiments on this head. . . . .

" I apprehend those only give a true account of the matter, who interpret the *tenth part of the city*, of the kingdom of *France*. Not that the latter calamities of the second woe will only affect that particular kingdom ; but also all those other kingdoms that have been for some time past, and that now are, and shall be, at war with them, in order to bring about the grand issue of this woe. And therefore it involves all the calamities that the house of Austria and her allies have, or may suffer, in the course of the present war, till France is *absolutely pulled down*. . . . .

" The reasons why expositors have been thus puzzled and divided on the present argument, I apprehend, have been principally these two.

" First, The *place* in which this account stands : namely, between the sixth and the seventh trumpet : for being assured it cannot belong to the seventh trumpet, which comprehends the *third woe*; they have naturally referred it to the events belonging to the sixth trumpet, as summarily included in the transactions of the second woe. In this general reference they have undoubtedly been right; but their mistake, I imagine has been here : that they have not distinguished between the *double* object of the second woe, or sixth trumpet; namely, its larger reference to the empire in general, and its

more

more reftrained application to fome particular kingdom in the empire. . . .

" Secondly, That the difficulties in this point have
been farther occafioned (and I take this to have
been the grand overfight), that none fo far as I
have feen have attended to the connection . . . between the 12th and 13th verfes of this eleventh
chapter; or between the *afcenficu* of the *witneffes*,
and the down'al of the *tenth part of the city*, appears
to me from that remarkable preface, by which the
accounts of the 13th verfe are introduced, in thefe
words, *And the fame hour*, &c. The queftion upon
this is, The *fame hour* with what? Take the anfwer from the preceding verfe: namely, *the fame
hour* with *the afcenfion of the witneffes*.—And that
there is a mutual connection between thofe events,
or that they reciprocally depend the one on the
other, is evident; becaufe the witneffes cannot
afcend till *the tenth part of the city* is overthrown;
and *the tenth part of the city* is no fooner overthrown, but the witneffes do *afcend*. The one is
introductory to the other.—And though the afcenfion of the witneffes is here placed antecedent to
the downfal of *the tenth part of the city*, the obvious
reafon is, becaufe it is proper in point of method,
and, I believe, is generally obferved through this
whole prophecy, to finifh all that concerns any one
branch of hiftory (or to give the feveral parts
making up any one whole fcene) before you proceed to another; notwithftanding the accounts in
the fucceeding paragraph or verfe, may be neceffary
to make way for the accomplifhment of what goes
before. Thus here St. John, having a vifion of
the witneffes, finifhes what relates to them, even to
their *afcenfion*, before he enters upon the fubverfion
of the *tenth part of the city*; though that event was

neceffary

neceffary to introduce the other. But their mutual
connection and dependence, as was obferved above,
is fufficient to account for any difficulty on this
head. When the *one falls*, the *other afcends*. Evident from hence—that the downfal of *the tenth
part of the city* is followed by a *revolution* in *ecclefiaftical* affairs, as well as *civil*.

" Now taking this connection along with us, I
think I may venture to fay, we have the true key
to the interpretation of this part of the fecond woe.
For, as it has an immediate reference to the witneffes, and is to iffue in that event, which confum-
mates their hiftory ; fo it points us to *the feat of
their fufferings*, and therein to the *feat of their glory* :
Providence ordering it fo, that *where* they were
flain, *there* alfo they fhall afcend. And that it is
moft probable FRANCE is the part particularly defigned for this tranfaction, will I hope, appear with
fome evidence, when I have given you

" II. Probable *reafons*, that *the tenth part of the
city* is defcriptive of the kingdom of FRANCE.

" 1. When the *old* Roman empire was broken
into *ten kingdoms*, by the inundations of the Goths
and Vandals, and other northern nations ; France
was the *laft* of thofe kingdoms in fucceffion and
eftablifhment.—It rofe after the nine, and fo made
up the complement of ten. It was properly *the
tenth* in order of rifing, and as fuch was the very
kingdom which completed the papal, antichriftian beaft ; I mean the *fecular* beaft, to which
the papacy, or *fecond beaft* with *two horns*, owes its
exiftence and fupport. Hence it is very obfervable, that the gold crown which Clovis, the firft
Chriftian king of France, fent to Rome, is ftill
called *Le Regne* [the kingdom] as much as to fay,
that they looked upon their kingdom, [that of the
fecular

fecular antichriftian beaft] as now completed, by this avowed acceffion of France.

" 2. As the kingdom itfelf was *the tenth*, in order of time or appearance; fo the name of the firft king of France that was Chriftian, and therefore, that fubmitted to the papal jurifdiction, includes in its *numerical letters*, the *number of the beaft*, 666; being, as the fcripture exprefsly fays, the *number of a man*; which is fo much the more remarkable, as that we herein obferve, that the number of the beaft has a double reference; not only fuggefting its *period* or *duration*, but alfo its *rife* or *completion*. —The name of this firft Chriftian king was CLO-DOVÆUS, which is only a corruption of, or another word for LUDOVICUS *. And therefore this is a grand clue for the leading us both to the com-mencement of the fecular antichriftian beaft, which muft be fome time in the reign of Clodovæus; and alfo to the conclufion of the papal power in this [the fecular] branch of it: its period of 1260 years, properly fpeaking, expiring with a *revolution* in this kingdom. But of this hereafter.

" 3. Another reafon for the prefent application is, that France, more lately, in its extent of do-minion, not only anfwers to *the tenth part* of the European fhare of the old Roman empire, but it is alfo for influence and power, the moft confiderable of all the other kingdoms, who originally confented to give their intereft to the beaft.—The French nation has been very formidable in itfelf, and al-ways forward to enter into the fervice of Rome: *fierce* and *bloody perfecutors of the proteftants*; to in-

---

* Clovis, Clodovic, Lewis, ou Luduin, car c'eft le MESME NOM, &c. Mezeray, Tom. I. Continuation de l'Hiftoire de France, &c. Liv. vi. p. 3. à Paris, 1652.

ftance

ftance only in the fingle reign of their late king Lewis XIV. in whom that black character of antichrift was but too eminently verified, namely, that *he fhould wear out the faints of the Moft High.* . . . As France therefore, in the times of the old Roman empire was called *The Province,* by way of eminence; fo is fhe ftill *the tenth,* on the fame principle, the grand prop of the antichriftian hierarchy. Again,

" 4. The *probability* of the prefent interpretation appears, in that the war has for fome time paft been on foot. . . . . Once more,

" It deferves our notice, that as France *was the laft of the ten kingdoms,* in which the fecular antichriftian beaft was completed; fo it is certain, it is now *the only one* that has not yet fuffered a *revolution:* what I mean is, has never been conquered in fuch manner, as that an *abfolute change of government* has fucceeded. It is, however, undeniable, that it muft become fuch a conqueft, before the papal antichrift can be removed: becaufe the fecular power muft be fet afide, before the ecclefiaftical can poffibly fink. And it is very probable, that Providence has fixed *the period of the firft,* (that is, the fecular beaft) in this kingdom, by telling us, that *the number of the beaft* is the *number of a man;* meaning, I fuppofe, *a number contained in the name of a man.* . . . . To intimate, I conceive, (befides what regards its original;) that the fecular beaft is to meet its *period in the downfal of this kingdom;* and that at a time when one of the *Lewis's* fhall fit on the throne.

" The *effects* attending the accomplifhment of this prophecy, is a farther indication, that the kingdom of France is immediately defigned by *the tenth part of the city.* Now the principal effects, or fuch

as

as we are directly furnifhed with from the text, are three; of which,

" The firft, as was intimated above, is already begun, being a means leading to the completion of this prophecy, *the flaughter of men of note*; yet more fully to be accomplifhed in giving the *finifhing blow* to this great work. . . . .

" The next remarkable effect is *a revolution in religious principles*, as well as fecular intereft. The text exprefsly tells us (as has likewife been obferved) that *the remnant were affrighted, and gave glory to the God of heaven*.—By the *remnant* we are undoubtedly to underftand thofe who fhall not be cut off in the downfal of *the tenth part of the city*, by the preceding war. And by their being *affrighted*, &c. we are evidently to conclude, that they become converts to pure and primitive chriftianity.—But it will be faid, where is there proof, that this is an event applicable to *a remnant* in the French nation? I anfwer, the evidence for it is this, ... becaufe *all the other* antichriftian ftates but France, have their particular judgments affigned them in a fucceeding chapter, viz. the xvth to take place under the effects of the *third woe*. Thofe therefore, notwithftanding the effects brought about by the *fecond woe* ftill continue papal in religion and government; while the *remnant* here become *truly* Chriftian, coalefce with the *two witneffes*, in their *remains*, and join with them in their triumphs, now immediately opening: which leads me to,

" The *laft* effect, namely, *the afcenfion of the witneffes*; that is, the deliverance of the Waldenfes and Albigenfes, in their *remains* [to be confidered, neverthelefs, not merely as the reprefentatives of the two antient, original witneffes; but alfo by virtue

tue of their defcent and profeffion, as actually the
prefent two witneffes againft the papal corruption,
yet in a wildernefs ftate : the deliverance of thefe,
the remains and fucceffors of the ancient Waldenfes
and Albigenfes] from the obfcurity and diftrefs
they are now in, with refpect to religious matters ;
and giving them an opportunity of making a *public*
profeffion of the pure Chriftian faith, for which
they have now fo, long fuffered from the French .
and their adherents; an opportunity to make this
profeffion *openly* and *boldly* in the kingdom of
France itfelf, the very feat of their moft cruel fufferings and [*political*] death.   With this additional
circumftance to their glory, and the mortification
of their former enemies, that they fhall do it, in
the fight of fuch other Roman catholic ftates, as
yet remain unconverted—And *their enemies beheld
them.*

" There are expofitors who are right as to the
true interpretation of the witneffes themfelves,
namely, that they intend the Waldenfes and Albigenfes, whofe original rife and feat, we are very
certain was France ; but then in the application of
the events concerning thefe witneffes, fuch particularly as their *afcenfion*, they very unhappily go off
from the point, ... and refer that to Chriftianity
in general, which the text abfolutely reftrains to
thefe particular witneffes.—But while we keep here,
the *effects* themfelves fix the feat of the calamities
intended by the fecond woe, immediately to France.
Others at war with them, to bring about this happy
revolution, as has been faid above, muft, for the
time, likewife fuffer with them ; but thofe only oc-
cafionally and collaterally ; the *immediate* feat of
action appears to be France : and that for the reafon now before us, namely, because as the original
of

of thofe Witneffes was FRANCE, as it was *here*, that they bore their *firft* teftimony againft the papal corruption: and again, as it was *here*, in the *remains* of both churches, that they principally fuffered; *here*, that they have *prophefied* in *fackcloth*, and laid concealed in a wildernefs condition; and finally, as it was *here*, and in the *Vallies* [of PIEDMONT] that they were *killed*, and here that they *rofe again*. As FRANCE, either at *firft* or *laft*, either *immediately*, or by her *tools*, has been ever remarkably concerned in *all* the *afflictions* and perfecutions, relative to thefe *two Witneffes*: fo it feems highly probable to conclude, that it fhall be likewife *here*, that thefe fame *Witneffes fhall afcend*; and that they are to afcend by, or upon the overthrow of thofe very enemies from whom they have principally fuffered: Providence, by this method, coming *home* to the perfecutors, and revenging *the quarrel* of his faithful Witneffes *on the fpot.*——But I have yet to fubjoin,

" 7. (Tho' it was covertly hinted at above,) that a farther reafon for the prefent application of the tenth part of the city to the kingdom of FRANCE, is, That unlefs fuch application be admitted, we fhall in vain feek for the execution of any *particular judgment* on that part of the fecular antichriftian beaft through the whole Revelation: which is an omiffion not only not to be accounted for, but, indeed, not to be fuppofed.——FRANCE has been always a remarkable limb, and notorious fupport of the papal idolatry, and therefore muft needs claim her fhare in the plagues referved for that hierarchy; nothing however of this kind will be found to occur, unlefs the deftruction here threatened on *the tenth part of the city*, be the thing fought for.

" Laftly, the prefent interpretation farther bids

H   fair

fair for the truth, forafmuch as the fall of Antichrift
himfelf (the Weftern or papal however) and therefore *moft* of, if not *all*, the grand events belonging to the *feventh trumpet*, feem to depend on *the
fubverfion of the tenth part of the city*.——FRANCE,
as has been obferved, is now the moft powerful of
all the catholic ftates, and therefore it is not at all
probable that the papacy fhould fall, till *that be
taken out of the way*. The very introduction of the
vials feems to depend on this event. . . . This, as I
take it, is the reafon, why the account of her ruin is
inferted in this particular place ; that is to fay, between the fixth and feventh trumpets ; feeming one
while to belong to the fixth, by being mentioned
under the fixth trumpet, and at another to belong
to the feventh, by being mentioned after *the
afcenfion of the witneffes* : to intimate, in fhort, as
appears to me, that it is the grand event *between*
both; clofing what concerns the *fecond woe* under
the *fixth trumpet*, and bringing on what belongs to
the third, under *the feventh*. . . .

" III. Of the EARTHQUAKE, how to be underftood, and what its effects.

" Having thus fix'd the object of the fecond woe,
in its latter branch, and made it probable, at leaft,
that FRANCE is more immediately the kingdom,
which is to fuffer by the *earthquake* here fpoken of.
This leads directly to inquire into the meaning of
that expreffion ; or what we are to underftand by
the term *earthquake*, in the prophetic ftyle.

" 1. Now we learn by former accounts in this
book where the fame expreffion is ufed, that it
intends remarkable commotions in a ftate or kingdom ; and fuch as are attended with a *revolution*
in the *body politic*, or *form of government*. Thus
particularly, with refpect to the *fixth feal* which
brought

brought on *the revolution* in the Roman empire,
under Conftantine the Great; the defcription opens
with this chara&ter: *and lo, there was a great earthquake.* So by the like term in this place, as
it affe&ts *the tenth part of the city,* we are doubtlefs
to underftand fuch *wars and commotions* in the
kingdom of FRANCE (allowing the premifes juft)
as will, at laft, iffue in *the diffolution* of the prefent
form of *government and the introduction* of a NEW
SYSTEM, both in *civil* and *ecclefiaftical matters,* within that dominion.

" 2: Not that I apprehend this is the *whole* intended by the *prefent term.* For as reference is here
had to *the witneffes,* and it is by *this event,* that
way is to be made for *their afcenfion* ; as there is in
the text, a fingular agreement between the POWER,
exercifed by the moft eminent of the prophets under the Old Teftament difpenfation and thefe *two
witneffes* under the New : and laftly, as the fame
extraordinary effe&ts are attributed to *this power,*
lodged with the prefent witneffes, with what were
produced by thofe prophets, and turned upon their
enemies : [*effects* big with *deftruction* to every fecular power, that attempts the extirpation *of the
witneffes.*] So it is not improbable, but that this
earthquake may likewife include fuch remarkable
occurrences in nature, preparatory to their laft general deliverance, as that the *ftars in their courfes* may
again be made to *fight againft their enemies.* . . .

" This conftru&tion of the word *earthquake,* as I
faid above, is founded chiefly on the extraordinary
influence or power affigned the *witneffes* in the
eleventh chapter ; nothing of which has yet been obferved to turn up in their hiftory, that I know of ;
and therefore is moft probably referved for the
times of this GRAND REVOLUTION,

No. XI. DR. GILL. 1748.

A VERY eminent and learned diffenting Minifter
among the baptift denomination, particularly diftinguifhed by his rabinical learning.

The following extract is taken from his elaborate
e pofition, in

" Rev. XI, 13. *And the fame hour was there a
great earthquake* [or *the fame day*, as the Complu-
tenfian edition, and fome copies, read] that is, at the
time of the refurrection and afcenfion of the witneffes, as there was at the refurrection of Chrift; and
is to be underftood of a very great commotion in
the civil affairs of kingdoms and nations within the
Roman jurifdiction, as there was when Rome Pagan
was near its ruin, chapter vi. 12. *And the tenth
part of the city fell* . . . . By the *city* is meant the
city of Rome the great city mentioned in verfe 8.
And by the *tenth part* of it may be defigned, either
Rome itfelf, which as it now is, according to the
obfervation of fome, is but a tenth part of what it
was once; fo that the fame thing is meant as when
it is faid, " Babylon is fallen, is fallen:" or, it may
defign the tithes and profits which arife from the
feveral kingdoms belonging to the jurifdiction and
fee of Rome, which now will fall off from thofe
who ufed to fhare them, upon this new and fpiritual
ftate of things, the gofpel daily gaining ground, and
enlightening the minds of men, and freeing them
from the flavery they were held in: or . . . rather,
one of the ten kingdoms into which the Roman
weftern empire was divided. *Dr. Goodwin* feems
inclined to think, that Great Britain is intended,
which having been gained over to the popifh party
will

will now fall off again: but I rather think the kingdom of FRANCE is meant, the laft of the ten kingdoms, which rofe up out of the ruins of the Roman empire, which will be conquered, and which will be the means of its reformation from popery.

" *And in the earthquake were flain of men feven thoufand.*

" The meaning is that in the commotions, maffacres, tumults and wars which will be throughout the empire fuch a number of men will be flain; which is either put for a greater number, a certain for an uncertain (as in Rom. xi. 4. and perhaps in reference to the account there) otherwife feven thoufand is but a fmall number to be flain in battle; or as it is in the original text, " *the* NAMES of MEN 7000" now it is obferved by fome, that the fmalleft name of number belonging to men is a centurion, or captain of an hundred men; and fuppofing that to be meant, then feven thoufand names of men will imply that in an hour, or a fortnight's time, may be flain throughout all Europe in battles and maffacres about 700,000 men which is a very large number: or NAMES *of men* may fignify *men of name,* of great renown (as in Numbers xvi. 2.) and then if feven thoufand men of name, officers in armies fhould be flain, how great muft be the number of the common foldiers? Some have thought that ECCLESIASTICAL DIGNITIES, or men diftinguifhed by NAMES and TITLES, fuch as cardinals, archbifhops, bifhops, priefts, and the whole rabble of the antichriftian hierarchy, which will now fall and be utterly demolifhed, are intended."

The following paffages are taken from a remarkable SERMON by Dr. Gill, on the *watchman's anfwer* to the queftion, *what of the night?*

" If it fhould be afked, What time it is with

us now? where-about we are? and what is yet to
come of this night? As a faithful watchman, I'll
give you the best account I can: I take it, we
are in the *Sardian* church-state, in the latter part
of it, which brought on the reformation, and
represents that; we are in the decline of that
state: and there are many things said of that
church which agree with us; as that we have a
name, that we *live*, and are *dead*; &c. . . . . .
it is a fort of a twilight with us, between clear and
dark, between day and night. As to what of the
night is yet to come, or what will befal the churches,
and will bring on the difmal night before us;
they are the flaying of the witneffes, and the univerfal fpread of popery all over Chriftendom; and
the latter is the unavoidable confequence of the
former.

" The *flaying of the witneffes*, which I underftand
not fo much in a literal fenfe, or of a corporal death;
though there may be many flain in this fenfe when
it will be; but in a civil fenfe, with refpect to their
miniftry, being filenced by their enemies, and neg-
lected by their friends; this is an affair that is not
yet over: . . . the witneffes have not yet *finifhed their
teftimony*; they are ftill *prophefying*, though *in fackcloth*, or under fome difcouragements; whereas it
will be when they have finifhed their teftimony, and
at the clofe of the 1260 days, or years of antichrift's
reign, that they will be *killed*.. the ruin of antichrift
will immediately follow the rifing and afcenfion of
thefe witneffes; for at the *fame hour* that they fhall
afcend, will be a great earthquake, or a REVOLUTION
in the papal ftate; and the tenth part of the city, or of
the Romifh jurifdiction, fhall fall; that is, one of its
ten horns, kings or kingdoms belonging to it, and
perhaps the kingdom of *France* is meant, and *feven
thoufand*

thoufand men of name will be flain, and the reft be
affrighted, and give glory to God; nothing of
which has yet been done.....From all of which it
may be concluded, that the flaying of the witneffes
is yet to come, and will make the difmal part
of that night we are entering into, and which will
be accompanied with a univerfal fpread of Popery :
.....but her *plagues fhall come in one day, death, and
mourning, and famine, and fhe fhall be utterly burnt
with fire*....Before the utter deftruction of antichrift,
he fhall go forth again *with great fury to deftroy,
and utterly to make away many*; yea, *he fhall plant
the tabernacles of his palace between the feas, in the
glorious holy mountain,* or *the mountain of delight, of
holinefs* ; and what place is there in all the globe, to
which this defcription fo well anfwers as *Great
Britain?* this will be done before, and but a little
before his ruin; for it follows, *yet he fhall come to
his end, and none fhall help him.*"

" Now, in all that I have faid upon the whole,
I do not pretend to any extraordinary impulfe
from God, or to any prophetic fpirit, but I ground
all upon the word of God; and if what I have faid
does not appear from thence, and upon the face of
things in providence, I have no pretenfions to any
thing elfe to fupport my opinion with, and as fuch
only I deliver it."

REMARKS

REMARKS ON THE PRECEDING EXTRACTS.

Our observations are designed by way of RECOL-
LECTION, REFLECTION, and IMPROVEMENT of the
subject.

I. By way of assisting the reader's RECOLLEC-
TION, we observe,

1. That these writers, on the authority of certain passages of scripture, predict a grand and important REVOLUTION in FRANCE—a change both
of the *ecclesiastical* and *civil polity*; the introduction
of a NEW SYSTEM, fatal to popery and tyranny, but
friendly to the liberty, peace and happiness of
mankind.

2. They foretel that this revolution shall be effected not in the ordinary course of things, nor by
the ministry of the gospel—but by a *peculiar dispensa-
tion* of heaven—by a sudden convulsion, compared to
an EARTHQUAKE; yet not (in the first instance at
least) attended with any great effusion of blood;
but the chief destruction shall be of NAMES, *titles,
ecclesiastical dignities, privileged orders,* &c. and attended with a great *humiliation* (at least) even of
Monarchy itself—and that this event should be introductory to a period in which religion and government should be reduced to a degree of primitive simplicity—in which the pride of courts, the
ambition of conquerors, and the deceits and usurp-
ation of ecclesiastical tyrants shall have no place.

3. They add, That the *ecclesiastical treasures* shall
be diverted into a new channel—That the French
nation shall break with Rome; not at once, but by
degrees—and thus a door be gradually opened for
the

the propagation of the gofpel in France and other parts of Europe.

4. (Thefe writers circumfcribe a period for thefe great events—between 1785 and 1795, fays *Jurieu* —between 1790 and 1794, fays *Fleming*—Our *Anonymous* writer, and feveral of the others fay, in the reign of a *Lewis*—and *Love* fays, *Babylon* (or popery) fhall *fall* (or begin to fall) in 1790.)

5. Befide the events which immediately relate to France, fome of the above mention a particular mortification of the houfe of *Auftria*—Others (as *Ufher* and *Gill*) fpeak of the flaying and refurrection of the witneffes in a manner not yet accomplifhed.—Our firft extract taken from Archbifhop *Brown*, refpecting the *Jefuits*, has been literally fulfilled.—The curfe of *John Knox* on the French king has been moft awfully accomplifhed in the fate of the unhappy Lewis XVI. in the third generation from the tyrant, falfely furnamed, the *Great*.

II. We now proceed to offer a few REFLEC- TIONS on thefe extraordinary paffages.

And, 1. It muft be confeffed that many of thefe conjectures, particularly refpecting France, have been remarkably verified in the late revolutions of that kingdom; both as to facts and dates. The circumftances are too notorious to need particularizing : I will only obferve that whatever may be thought of the recent conduct of the French (and I am not their apologift) it will generally be admitted that many of the principles on which the new conftitutions have been erected, are not only novel and unprecedented, but in other refpects ftrongly correfpond with the characters above given.

2. It muft be admitted that all thefe good men have been more or lefs miftaken in feveral events

I   and

and circumstances of an *inferior* importance; and some of them in the periods they fixed for their fulfilment. Most of them have spoken only by way of conjecture, and made no pretensions to a spirit of prophecy. *Jurieu*, indeed, in the main of his predictions, believed himself under a *superior guidance*; and those very predictions have been wonderfully accomplished. It may be objected, that he, with some of the others, was unhappily mistaken as to the French revolution producing little or no bloodshed: but it should be observed that in the first instance this was wonderfully true. It was the interference of foreign powers afterward, and the violence of domestic parties, which produced the horrid slaughter which succeeded; and which offers another awful fulfilment of the prophecy, by destroying a prodigious *number* of *men* of *name*, title, fame and quality.)

3. It is not impossible, however, that some of the above conjectures, not hitherto fulfilled, may yet be so, in a manner as remarkable as any of the others. I will venture in one instance to point out the possibility of this.

Great and wonderful are the events now transacting on the theatre of Europe; and what will be the issue, it may be both vain and presumptuous to conjecture. But should the *combined powers* succeed in the *restoration of Monarchy* on a constitution similar to that of 1789 and 1790, we may see, as *Jurieu* conjectured, the French Monarchy raised again from its late humiliation, to new and unprecedented glory.—Or, should the *republic* acquire a peaceable establishment, if not the monarchy, yet the nation may obtain that dignity, which, perhaps, may equally comport with sacred prophecy.

Some have indeed expressed a fear lest the *ancient tyranny*

tyranny (ecclefiaftical as well as civil) fhould gain a re-eftablifhment in France—the dormant fpirit of *perfecution* be revived, and that general and dreadful flaughter of the *witneffes* follow, which was long fince expeéted by *Ufher*, and more recently by Dr. *Gill*. The Lord avert from us fuch a judgment! But, even in this cafe, we have the confolation to be fatisfied, both from prophecy and from circumftances, that fuch a triumph muft be very tranfient, and immediately introduce a better ftate of things than the world has yet experienced. A permanent tyranny in France can hardly be expeéted by thofe who wifh to exercife it ; and by others I hope not defired.

4. It may be enquired in what light are we to confider thefe extraéts?—Certainly not as a *new* revelation, and not *merely*, I conceive, as happy *gueffes*. But as *rational conjeétures* on the *fcripture prophecies*, which form a powerful argument in favor of divine revelation. For unlefs the reader confider all thefe as random gueffes, or admit them as new revelations, either of which I fuppofe few will do, it muft follow, that they are juft explications of exifting prophecies ; and confequently, that thofe prophecies have been *accomplifhed.)* Now the accomplifhment of prophecy is the proper evidence of its infpiration: and in this view we have acquired from the events of our own times, an additional and ftriking evidence of the truth of holy fcripture.

5. I fhall only add a remark that may be of fome ufe in appreciating the value of thefe authors—They are not all *equally originals*; Dr. *Goodwin*, and Monf. *Jurieu*, feem to have been moft eminently fo: But it is highly probable that Mr. *Fleming* had feen both thefe authors ; and Dr. *Gill*,

Gill, and perhaps the *Anonymous* writer, all the three. This is not meant to depreciate the latter writers; but to affist the reader in forming a comparative eftimate of the extracts.

III. We shall now beg leave to attempt fome practical IMPROVEMENT of the subject, by remarking the conduct of Divine *Providence*, in the events above alluded to.

When the Prophet *Ezekiel* [chap i.] entered on his miffion he was, for his inftruction and encouragement favoured with one of the fublimeft vifions that can be conceived; in which are many particulars which perplex the ableft commentators; but the geneial defign appears to be, that the whole was intended to exhibit, in the *wheels*, an idea of the *machinery* of Divine Providence; and by the *cherubim*, the *agency* by which it is conducted. In this view, the following hints I hope will not be thought impertinent, though not offered as a complete explanation of the vifion.

1. In this scenery we may obferve the *magnificence* of Providence. Not to advert to the flaming cherubim or fapphire-coloured throne, how magnificent the machine itfelf! *The rings were fo high,* faith the prophet, *that they were dreadful* to behold, their *colour* was like the *beryl*, (i. e.) a beautiful fea green, and they were *full of eyes* round about. The prodigious circumference of the wheels, reprefents the comprehenfivenefs of Providence, the magnitude of its objects, and the grandeur of its movements; but the *eyes* fuggeft another idea, namely,

2. The *wifdom* of Providence. Chance is properly reprefented blind, but Providence is full of eyes. It is alfo faid, that *the spirit of the living creatures*, or the fame fpirit that actuates them,

resideth

refideth *in the wheels*, and directeth all their motions; and while worldly men rely on the fagacity of their ftatefmen, or the prudence of their generals, he fruftrates the counfels of an *Abitophel*, and *taketh the wife in their own craftinefs.*—But this circumftance may intimate alfo,

3. The *harmony* of Providence—the fame *fpirit* refideth both in the living creatures and in the wheels, and thus directs the whole machinery, and fecures the moft perfect harmony in all its movements—" when the living creatures went, the wheels went by them; and when the living creatures were lifted up from the earth, the wheels were lifted up.—Whitherfoever the fpirit was to go, they went."

4. The *irrefiftibility* of Providence is ftrongly implied both in the magnitude of the wheels, which were *terrible* to behold, and in the power by which they were directed, the fpirit that was in them. Hence they went *ftraight forward*, no obftacle could change their courfe; they *turned not as they went*, no power could impede their motion—for they, as well as the living creatures, " ran and returned, as the appearance of a flafh of lightning."

5. This machinery reprefents the *myfterioufnefs* of divine Providence—it was as if it were *a wheel within a wheel*, i. e. feveral rings involved one in another, like the circles of an armillary fphere: fo complicated are the movements of Providence. We behold indeed the revolutions of the machine, but know nothing of the mechanifm (fo to fpeak) within. Hence are we often deceived in calculating events and confequences, by our own fagacity. But *prophecy* is like the *index* of the clock; by its neceflary connection with the internal movements—by its being dictated by *the*

fpirit

spirit that refideth *in the wheels*—it becomes, as far as we are enabled to underftand it, a certain guide to our conjectures. But without this how vain and uncertain are all political fpeculations! When the Duke of Brunfwick marched with the flower of his army into the heart of France—When the armies of the republic fpread thir victories thro' all the furrounding countries—or, when on a fudden turn of affairs, Dumourier declared for monarchy, and marched back to France with a view to effect a counter-revolution—what power feemed able to withftand them?—None; but that of the

> * * * * * * * " Hand unfeen
> " Which guides and turns the great machine."

an idea in perfect coincidence with the vifion of the prophet, who obferved that every living creature had the *hand* as *of a man* concealed beneath his wings.

Once more, 6. When Ezekiel had a repetition of the vifion (ch. x. 13.) a voice, I fuppofe from the celeftial throne, proclaimed to the machine—not " O wheel," as in our tranflation, being quite a different word from that rendered *wheel* in the context—but rather—" REVOLUTION *."—As if to inform us that the proper defign and tendency of the wheels, is to effect REVOLUTIONS as well in nations and communities, as in the affairs of families and individuals. The world fubfifts by *revolutions*. Good men, indeed, fhould be cautious of promoting fuch as are needlefs; and may tremble at the moft neceffary: but if the voice from heaven cry,

---

* See Parkhurft's Heb. Lex. in בן.

RE-

" REVOLUTION!" in vain would all the powers upon earth attempt to arreſt the motions of theſe wheels. They ſhall go round till every ſacred prediction is accompliſhed; till the laſt event in the plan of Providence is brought to paſs.

It is certain that the authors of the French revolution had nothing leſs in view than the accompliſhment of prophecy; yet had this been their only deſign they could not have done it more effectually.) It is the Lord's uſual method to effect his purpoſes by undeſigning, and even *refractory* agents. *He doth whatſoever pleaſeth him,* not only *in the armies of heaven*; but alſo *among the inhabitants of the earth.*

It is indeed ſhocking to think of the preſent ſlaughter amongſt conflicting powers and parties; but prophecy holds out this conſolation, that when the *judgment written* ſhall be accompliſhed, and the preſent convulſions ſubſide—*the remnant ſhall give glory to the God of heaven*—ſhall acknowledge his hand in all their ſufferings; and, I hope, receive his goſpel in all its purity and power.

THE END.

Juft Publifhed by W. BUTTON, No. 24, Paternofter Row.

INFANT SALVATION:

An Effay to prove the Salvation of all who die in Infancy: with Anfwers to Objections. Written with a particular View to the Confolation of bereaved Parents. Price Six Pence.

THE ASSEMBLY's CATECHISM ABRIDGED,

For the Ufe of Children, particularly in the *Sunday Schools*; with felect Proofs, and fhort explanatory Notes from Dr. Watts. Recommended by the Rev. Meffrs. Burder, Clayton, Crole, Jay, Ralph, Towers, Upton, and Dr. E. Williams. Price Two Pence, with Allowance to give away.

Subfcribers Names continue to be received by W. Button, on behalf of the fame Author, for the following Work, which is preparing for the Prefs (in two Pocket Volumes, Price 5s.)

AN HISTORIC DEFENCE

OF

EXPERIMENTAL RELIGION.

In which the Doctrine of *Divine Influences* is particularly confidered, and fupported by the Authority of Scripture, and the *Experience* of the wifeft and beft Men in all Ages and Countries.